A CAJUN TALL TALE

Feliciana Feydra Le Roux

by Tynia Thomassie

Illustrated by Cat Bowman Smith

Little, Brown and Company

Boston   New York   Toronto   London

In celebration of my grampa, Clarence Eustev Thomassie
T. T.

In memory of Gretchen, who led us from a lake's cracking ice,
pulled K'nada from quicksand, and shut the gate on stampeding cows
C. B. S.

Text copyright © 1995 by Tynia Thomassie
Illustrations copyright © 1995 by Cat Bowman Smith

First Paperback Edition

Library of Congress Cataloging-in-Publication Data

Thomassie, Tynia.
    Feliciana Feydra LeRoux : a Cajun tall tale / by Tynia Thomassie ; illustrated by Cat Bowman Smith.
    — 1st ed.
        p.   cm.
    Summary: Even though Feliciana is her grandfather's favorite, he refuses to allow her to go alligator
hunting with him, so one night she sneaks out and surreptitiously joins the hunt anyway.
    ISBN 0-316-84125-0 (hc)
    ISBN 0-316-84459-4 (pb)
    [1. Louisiana — Fiction. 2. Alligators — Fiction. 3. Cajuns — Fiction.]
I. Smith, Cat Bowman, ill. II. Title.
PZ7.T36967Fe   1995
[E] — dc20   93-30347

10 9 8 7 6 5 4 3 2 1

WOR

Published simultaneously in Canada by Little, Brown & Company (Canada) Limited

Printed in the United States of America

Author's Note

What exactly is a Cajun? Well, Cajun people are natives of southern Louisiana. Their ancestors were exiled from Acadia, Canada, during the 1700s. (The term *Cajun* comes from the word *Acadia*.) This part of Canada had been a French colony, but when it was taken over by the British, some Acadians, who were proudly French, refused to take an oath of loyalty to the British crown and refused to give up their Catholic religion. They were driven from the colony and were pushed farther and farther down the Mississippi River. They ended up isolated in the southernmost swamps of Louisiana, where they were able to freely practice their religion and live by fishing, trapping, and fur trading.

Like any people who live primarily off the land, Cajuns use all parts of animals they hunt. For example, they really do go alligator hunting in the fall (as described in this story); the hides are used for clothing and shoes, and the meat from the tail is eaten. Cajun cooking features other unusual catch found in the bayou, such as crawfish, catfish, and frog's legs, blended in tasty sauces with hot spices. Music is an important part of Cajun life, too, and their special mix of instruments such as the accordion and the fiddle creates lively rhythms that invite dancing along. Their language is a unique combination of French and quirky twists of English phrases, spoken with a distinctive accent.

Cajun culture has remained relatively unchanged by the course of time. (In case you were wondering, *Feliciana Feydra LeRoux* is an original tale that takes place in the present.) Down-to-earth people who usually come from large families, the Cajuns generally prefer their traditional ways. But they would welcome anyone to "pass a good time" in their company.

A Cajun Glossary and Pronunciation Guide

The dialogue in this book is written as it would sound in Cajun country. You can use the pronunciation guide below and the Recipe for a Cajun Accent on the back cover to help you read the story like a true Cajun!

Adele (ah-DEL)

Albert (al-BARE)

bayou (BY-oo)
An inlet of a lake or small branch of a river; found throughout the marshes of Louisiana

Cajun two-step
A dance performed with a partner cheek-to-cheek; a two-step combination to a 4/4 beat

Celeste (say-LEST)

chère (shaa)
French for *dear;* used by Cajuns, with their own distinctive pronunciation, as a term of endearment

chinchilla
A squirrel-like rodent bred for its soft gray fur

jolie (joh-LEE; with a soft *j* sound, as in *rouge*)
French for *pretty;* used by Cajuns as a term of endearment

LeRoux (luh-ROO)

mais (may)
French for *but*

Memère (m'MARE)
Mother, from the French for *my mother*

mon coeur (moh^n cur)
French for *my heart*

nutrias
Otterlike rodents hunted for their fur

Octave (awk-TAVE)

parish
Louisiana equivalent of a county

pecan (p'KAW^n)

pirogue (PEE-rohg)
A hollowed log that serves as a canoe; steered with a paddle or a pole

Renee (ruh-NAY)

sacré Dieu! (SAH-kray dyuh)
French exclamation meaning "Holy God!"; Cajuns give the pronunciation their own flavor

sauce piquant (sahs pee-KAW^n)
A very spicy gravy common to Cajun cooking

seining (SAYN-ing)
A method of fishing in shallow water with a weighted net

shucking an oyster
Breaking open an oyster shell at its hinge with a shucking knife

sucking the heads of crawfish
Cajuns peel crawfish, eat the meat of the tail, and suck the hollow heads to enjoy the tasty fat and juice they draw while boiling — considered a delicacy

tail end of the LeRoux crew
The youngest child of the LeRoux family

'squita
Mosquito; fine netting is often draped over beds to protect a sleeper from mosquito bites

teetsie-walla (teet-see-wah-LAH)
A pet name like *cutie-pie*

ti (tee)
From the French *petit,* meaning "little"; used as a Cajun prefix, as in *ti-Jean,* to mean *Jr.*

ti-Jacques (tee-JAHK; with a soft *j* sound, as in *rouge*)

ti-Jean (tee-JAW^n; with a soft *j* sound, as in *rouge*)

ti-Juste (tee-JOOST; with a soft *j* sound, as in *rouge*)

Deep in the depths of Cajun country,
in a shack on stilts by the bayou,
lived a little girl known by the name of
Feliciana Feydra LeRoux.

Now, let me tell you something
about Feliciana Feydra.
She was the tail end of the LeRoux crew,
just like Grampa Baby was before he grew up to be
the oldest LeRoux.
Maybe that's why they were tied special together.

Of all the grandchildren — and there were plenty —
Feliciana Feydra was Grampa Baby's teetsie-walla.
Hoooo, he spoiled her rotten!

He jellied her toast with blackberry preserves to the very edges of the bread.

He passed her the heart of the artichoke after all the leaves were gone.

Why, he even let her suck the heads of his crawfish, now you know!

And the things he *made* for her! Mmmm-mmm-mmm!

He whittled her the finest fishing rod in all the parish.
He made her boots from armadillo hide to keep her tootsies dry from the marsh.
But the loveliest thing Grampa Baby ever made her was a doll from the wood of a pecan tree.
He spent weeks carving and shaping that baby doll, and Feliciana never parted with it.

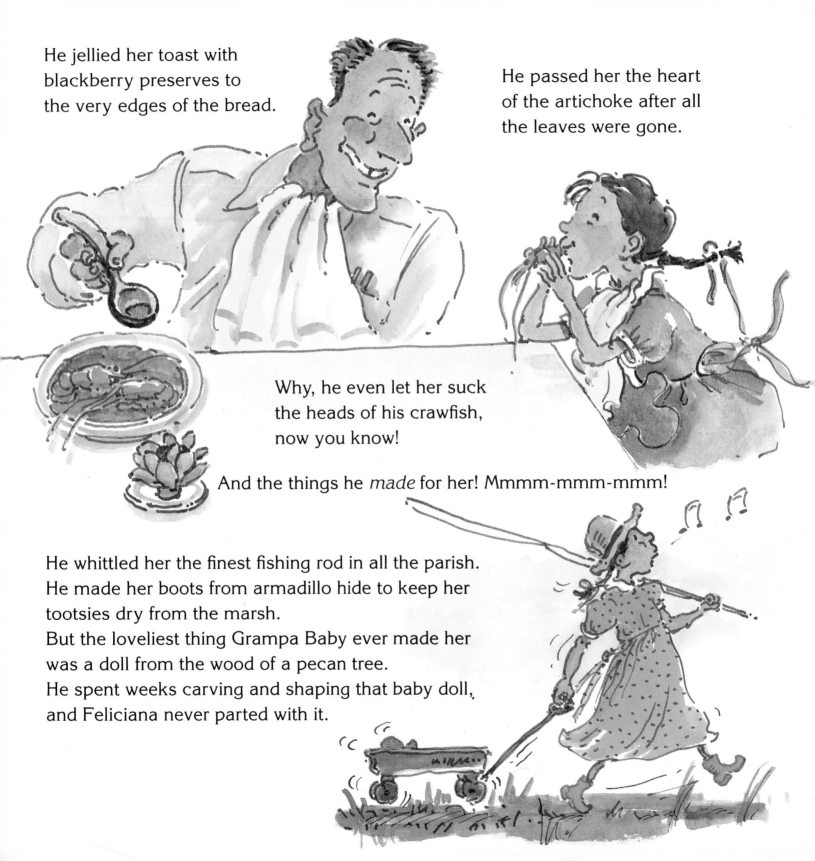

Grampa Baby took Feliciana fishing with him —
crabbing,
seining.

He taught her how to
Cajun two-step,
how to skin a chinchilla,
and how to shuck an oyster
faster than you can say
"*sauce piquant.*"

Wherever Grampa Baby was,
Feliciana Feydra was a heel behind.
That child was the apple in Grampa
Baby's eyes, and whatever she
wanted, she got!

But there was one thing even Grampa Baby wouldn't allow:
he never took her alligator hunting
(and it wasn't because she didn't ask!).

"Po-leez! P'leez lemme go halligator huntin' wi'choo, Grampa Baby,"
Feliciana would beg.

"I cain' see dat!" Grampa Baby'd say with his arms firmly folded.

You see, every October, Grampa Baby packed up all the men-children —

ti-Jean,

ti-Juste,

ti-Jacques,

Renee,

Octave,

an' Albert —

and as soon as the bayou would swallow the sun,
they'd drive off into the night, leaving Feliciana pouting on the porch
amidst the fireflies.

But this year Feliciana decided she wouldn't be left behind — no!
She decided to try a different tackle on the problem.

As the boys packed their gear in the truck, Feliciana hopped in the back of the truck, too.

"*Mais,* you ain't comin' wid us, no," said ti-Jean.

"Am, too," she said.

"You a *girl,* Feliciana," said ti-Juste.

"You a *shrimp,*" said ti-Jacques.

"You too much trouble," said Renee.

"Whoever heard o' takin' a baby doll on a halligator hunt!" said Octave.

Hooo, but the boys yucked it up!

Feliciana Feydra stomped her feet.

"You leave my doll outta dis! I can outsmart an ol' halligator any ol' day, an' I can outsmart all y'all to boot!"

"Whooa, all o' y'all!" shouted Grampa Baby
as he scooped Feliciana off the truck.
"It's got nothin' to do wid 'girl' o' 'size'"
— although Feliciana expected it *did* —
"You gotta hunt halligator in d'pitch-black night . . .
in d'swamps. It's too dangerous, *jolie.*"

"Why ain't it too dangerous for d'boys?"
demanded Feliciana.

"I couldn't take d'chance, *chère* —
you'd be too temptin' to a halligator,
bein' so sweet an' delicious."

Then with a great commotion,
Memère spun Feliciana round one way
and said, "Feliciana, help Celeste shell
some pecans for tomorrow's pie."

And sister Adele spun her
round the other way and said,
"Feliciana, I need your help
pickin' scraps for my quilt."

And before you could say "halligator," Grampa Baby and the boys were
driving away in the dark.

H'man, you could have hung your hat on that child's lower lip, I'm a tol' y'all.

That night Feliciana lay under the mosquito netting of her four-poster bed,
hating everybody.
She watched a mosquito dance near the candle flame next to her bed,
before it dashed out the window into the night.
Then she sprung straight up in bed.

"If a 'squita can come an' go as 'e pleases, I can, too," she decided.

Feliciana slipped her boots on under her nightgown, grabbed a flashlight
and her precious pecan baby doll, and followed the mosquito out the window
to the edge of the swamp.

One of her brothers' empty pirogues was tied to a tree on the bank.
Feliciana slid inside, then shoved off, poling her way through the swamp in silence —
under the cypress trees, through the moss,
past the nutrias lit by the grace of the moon.

The crickets clacked; the frogs, they moaned. Once in a while a fish
would flap, but mostly 'twas still. Feliciana sat perched alert as an owl,
looking for some trace of Grampa Baby and the boys . . .
when a high-pitched screech split the still in two!

And as the draping moss parted open above her head . . .
she threw on her flashlight!

Eye level with the water were two red eyes, froze-fix in the light. The alligator!

It was Feliciana's turn to freeze. Her fingers clamped a stranglehold about her pecan doll's neck. Her toes gripped the soles of her armadillo boots, and her tongue jammed up in the back of her mouth, as the two red eyes floated closer toward her. "Grampa Baby, where *are* you?" she whispered.

Like an answer to a prayer, a familiar shout floated back across the dark swamp: "*Sacré Dieu!*" screamed Grampa Baby. "Dat gator's eyein' my lil' girl. Boys, hold your fire — no matter what!"

Feliciana looked up and saw the moon-outlined figures of her brothers and Grampa Baby on their flatboat. They were only an arm's throw away! Grampa Baby lifted his lasso in the air to rope the gator's snout, but that gator turned sharp, opened his mouth W - I - D - E, and caught the rope in his jagged teeth. Them two had a fierce tug-a-war, but that gator got in one good jerk, and Grampa Baby plunged headfirst into the water.

H'man, that gator was thinking he was gonna have a good meal tonight.
But Feliciana Feydra felt her pecan baby doll in her hand,
and had another thought in mind.

"Oh, yoooo-hoo! Mr. Haaaalligator!" she shouted,
sticking out her tongue and shaking her fanny.
"Hey, y'ol' halligator, look at *me!*"

Then she kicked off her armadillo boots,
and with her pecan doll in tow, *dove* into the murky water!

Just that quick, that gator forgot about Grampa Baby
and swam toward filet o' Feliciana.

Hooo, that gator was *hungry!*
He opened his mouth, ready to swallow Feliciana whole.

But she rammed her pecan doll upright between his teeth and locked open his jaw!

Now, Feliciana's hootin' and hollerin' gave Grampa Baby a chance to scramble back up on the flatboat.
He and the boys frantically poled toward Feliciana and the alligator, shouting, "Hang on, Feliciana! Hang on!"

While that gator flipped this way and that, fighting the pecan doll jammed in his mouth, Grampa Baby and the boys snuck up from behind and *struck* him on the snout and head with the butts of their guns.
Whoa, was Feliciana surprised when that pecan doll shot out of those teeth like a good tobacco spit and flew straight into her hands!

As the gator sank below the water, Feliciana ran right up his back like a staircase and jumped into the arms of Grampa Baby.

Hoooo, but Grampa Baby and the boys had never seen anything like *that* before, I wanna tell y'all. That LeRoux clan hooped and hollered with joy!

The next morning at the crack of dawn, as the sun was stretching wide above the bayou, Memère ran out to the porch to find the boys opening the back of the truck.

A big alligator tail plopped out, and there, straddled over its back like a cowgirl, was Feliciana Feydra LeRoux, grinning from ear to ear.

"Oh, *mon coeur!*" screamed Memère, clasping her heart.
"What do I see!"

Feliciana jumped off the truck and said,
"Look what we caught, Memère!"

"Feliciana Feydra LeRoux,
you get yo' hawd-headed fanny in dis house —
you and I are gonna tangle now! Your Grampa Baby forbid you
to go huntin' wid him, and you up an' defied him!"

"*Mais,* Grampa Baby wouldn' be alive if Feliciana hadn't saved d'day!"
said ti-Jean.
"Feliciana saved Grampa Baby from d'belly o' d'beast wid her pecan baby doll!"
said ti-Juste.

"Aw, dis is a tall tale y'all tellin' me now," said Memère with disgust.

"*Mais,* 'course it's fo' real, Memère," snorted Feliciana.

"Jus' looka my baby doll all chewed up in d'head!"

"H'well, I'll be," said Memère.

"How 'bout I make my girl a new baby doll?" offered Grampa Baby.

"Not fo' me, no!" Feliciana exclaimed. "I'm keepin' dis one so I can always 'member d'night I went halligator huntin'.

But I t'ink you should make y'own doll to hunt wid next time, Grampa Baby."

"Why? Aren't you two comin' wid us?"

"We'll pass!" she said with a wink. "You jus' too much trouble!"

Hooo, that LeRoux crew was so tickled about the big beast Feliciana
helped to catch that they invited their neighbors to share their good fortune.
Grampa Baby picked up his fiddle, and with their bellies full of alligator tail
and their hearts rich with each other, those Cajuns passed a good time.

Y'all pass a good time tonight, too, ya hear?